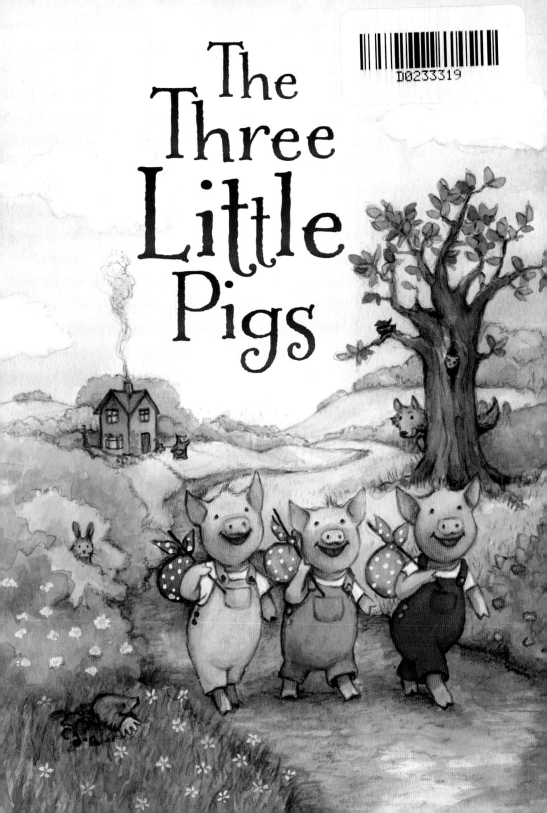

The Three Little Pigs

Once upon a time there were three little pigs. It was a big day for the little pigs because they were leaving home for the first time.

"Be careful, my little piggy-wigs," said Mother Pig, kissing each little pig on its chinny, chin, chin.

"Don't trust the **big bad wolf**. He will eat you if he gets the chance!"

6

The three little pigs set off down the road.
Soon they met a boy selling straw.

"I can use this straw to build myself a house,"
said the first little pig.

"Please can I buy some of your straw?"
he asked the boy.

So the first little pig planned to build his
house from straw.

"This will be a lovely, comfy house!"
said the first little pig.

"I am sure I will be
happy here!"

The other little pigs carried on down the road. Soon they met a girl selling wood.

"I can use this wood to build myself a house," said the second little pig.

"Please can I buy some of your wood?" he asked the girl.

So the second little pig started to build his house from wood.

"This will be a warm, cosy house!" said the second little pig.

"I am sure I will be happy here!"

The third little pig carried on down the road. Soon he met a man selling bricks.

"I can use these bricks to build myself a house," said the third little pig.

"Please can I buy some of your bricks?" he asked the man.

So the third little pig started to build his house from bricks.

"This will be a good strong house!" said the third little pig.

"I am sure I will be happy here!"

The three little pigs were very happy.
They were so busy finishing their houses
that they did not see the **big bad wolf**
spying on them from the bushes.

The **big bad wolf** licked his lips
when he saw the three little pigs.

He wanted to eat them!

The next day the **big bad wolf** went to visit the first little pig. He tapped lightly on the door.

"Little pig, little pig, let me come in!" said the **big bad wolf**.

"Not by the hair on my chinny, chin, chin! I will not let you in!" said the first little pig.

"Then I'll **huff** and I'll **puff** and I'll **blow your house down!**"
said the **big bad wolf**.

So he huffed and he puffed, and he blew the straw house down!

The little pig ran just in time to his brother's house, and escaped from the **big bad wolf**! 17

The next day the **big bad wolf** went to
visit the second little pig. He knocked loudly
on the door.

"Little pig, little pig, let me come in!"
said the **big bad wolf**.

"Not by the hair on my chinny, chin, chin!
I will not let you in!" said the second little pig.

"Then I'll **huff** and I'll **puff** and I'll **blow your house down!**" said the **big bad wolf**.

So he huffed and he puffed, and he blew the wooden house down!

The little pigs ran to their brother's brick house, and managed to escape from the **big bad wolf**!

19

The next day the **big bad wolf** went to
visit the third little pig. He banged hard on
the door.

"Little pig, little pig, let me come in!"
said the **big bad wolf**.

"Not by the hair on my chinny, chin, chin!
I will not let you in!" said the third little pig.

"Then I'll **huff** and I'll **puff** and I'll **blow** **your house down!"** said the **big bad wolf**.

So he huffed and he **puffed**, and he **huffed** and he **puffed** again ... but he could not blow the brick house down!

Then the **big bad wolf** had an idea ...

he could cl_imb do_wn the chimney!

On to the roof he jumped, quick as a flash!

But the third little pig had an idea too ...

He put a large pot of
hot water on the fire!

When the wolf came down the chimney,
he went SPLASH into the water!
It burned his bottom and he went running
out of the door never to be seen again.

Then the three little pigs all lived happily ever after!

Can you remember?

Now that you have read the story, try
to answer these questions about it.

1. Why was Mother Pig
   worried when she said
   goodbye to the three
   little pigs?

2. Who did the three little pigs meet first of all?

3. What did the **big bad wolf** say when
   he blew on each little pig's house?

"I'll ? and I'll ? and I'll ? your house down!"

4. Which little pig built
   his house from bricks?

5. The **big bad wolf**
   fell into a pot of …

Hot water?
OR
Cold soup?

Did you spot?

The **big bad wolf** was not the only one watching the three little pigs – other animals saw them too. See if you can find them all.

1. Can you see any rabbits grazing in the fields?

2. What about the two helpful mice?

3. Can you find all seventeen sheep in the fields?

4. Did you spot the squirrels watching the pigs?

5. How about the two robins?

6. The three little pigs did not see the **big bad wolf** watching them. When did you first spot him spying on them?

"Psst... I might appear earlier than you first think!"

True or false?

Can you answer these true or false questions correctly?

1. The straw house was the strongest.
True or false?

2. The third little pig built his house from bricks.
True or false?

3. When the **big bad wolf** huffed and puffed, the little pigs fell down.
True or false?

4. The **big bad wolf** lived happily ever after.
True or false?

5. "I'm a good wolf."
True or false?

Such a puzzle ...

Look carefully at the pictures below
and then try to answer the questions.

?

1. What is different about this
   picture of the three little pigs?

2. What was the
   big bad wolf's
   idea?

?

3. What was the third
   little pig doing in
   this part of the story?

Complete your collection ...